A Funeral in the Bathroom

and Other School Bathroom Poems

Kalli Dakos

pictures by
Mark Beech

Albert Whitman & Company
Chicago, Illinois

Library of Congress Cataloging-in-Publication Data

Dakos, Kalli.
A funeral in the bathroom : and other school bathroom poems /
by Kalli Dakos ; illustrated by Mark Beech.
p. cm
1. School children—Juvenile poetry. 2. School
buildings—Restrooms—Juvenile poetry. 3. Children's poetry, American.
I. Beech, Mark. II. Title.
PS3554.A414F86 2011
811'.54—dc22
2010045591

Text copyright © 2011 by Kalli Dakos
Pictures copyright © 2011 by Albert Whitman & Company
Pictures by Mark Beech
Hardcover edition published in 2011 by Albert Whitman & Company
Paperback edition published in 2017 by Albert Whitman & Company
ISBN 978-0-8075-2676-7

Printed in China
10 9 8 7 6 5 4 3 2 1 LP 20 19 18 17 16

Design by Carol Gildar

For more information about Albert Whitman & Company,
visit our website at www.albertwhitman.com.

For these amazing educators I am fortunate to know:
Carol Colip, Lois Copis, Sid Cratzbarg, Julia Critchfield,
Alex Dakos, Sylvia Digby, Dr. Eleanor Fall, Linda Fletcher, Tricia Gibbons,
Nancy Henderson, Susan Hogan, Eowana Jordan, Angela Kusulas, Ted Kusulas,
Athena Ladman, Mary McCoy, Sylvia Musselthwite, Carol Olson, Jan Price,
Ellen Rosenbloom, Rose Skrapits, Kathy Sperdakos, Lori Spiro, Jeanette Tabb,
and Brenda Tennant—KD

To my lovely niece Robyn, who is always smiling—MB

Contents

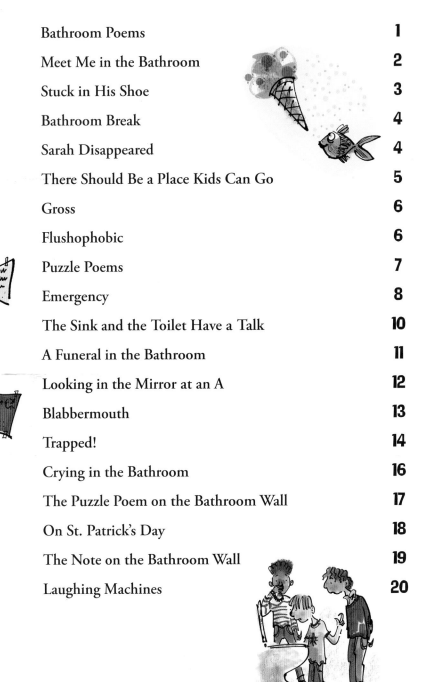

Bathroom Poems

My teacher's pretty slick,
has a hundred teaching tricks.

Even in the bathroom stalls,
she hangs poetry on the walls.

And while I'm there all alone,
I can't help but read a poem.

And then one day I realize
all the poems I've memorized:

happy, joyous, silly, glad,
funny, wondrous, grieving, sad,

rhyming, free verse, and quatrains,
all have seats inside my brain.

And today when I get home,
I plan to write this very poem,

about the teacher who's pretty slick
and has a hundred teaching tricks.

Meet Me in the Bathroom

Meet me in the bathroom,
right at two o'clock.
You leave your class,
I'll leave mine,
we'll have a chance to talk.

Meet me in the bathroom,
fake a stomachache.
You leave math,
I'll leave art,
we'll take a bathroom break.

Meet me in the bathroom,
I'll be waiting there for you.
On the trash can
by the sink,
at the dot of two.

Stuck in His Shoe

He didn't have
a single clue
when the toilet paper
stuck to his shoe.

And followed him
in a loooooooooong line
down the hall
past the office sign,

and right into
our spelling class,
where everyone

laughed

and laughed

and laughed!

Bathroom Break

Bathroom break,
tinkle time,

have a little
resting time.

Have a little
quiet time.

Bathroom break,
tinkle time.

Sarah Disappeared

Sarah disappeared
into the bathroom
an hour ago
with the novel
she was reading,

and we haven't
seen her since!

There Should Be a Place
Kids Can Go

There should be a place
kids can go
when life has dealt
another blow.

There should be a shuttle
to hitch a ride
into the dark
when we need to hide.

There should be a garden
or a room to pray
when pets die
and friends move away.

There should be a tree
kids can climb
when life is a poem
that's lost its rhyme.

When life is a poem
that's lost its rhyme,
kids head to the bathroom
all the time.

Gross

It isn't hard to diagnose
that a toilet's job
is rather gross.

Flushophobic

A girl in kindergarten
won't flush the toilet.

We think she might be

flushophobic!

Puzzle Poems

Puzzle poems,
puzzle poems,
on the bathroom walls.
Puzzle poems,
puzzle poems,
hanging in the stalls.

Puzzle poems,
puzzle poems,
Teacher put them there.
Puzzle poems,
puzzle poems,
hanging everywhere.

Puzzle poems,
puzzle poems,
by the bathroom sink.
Puzzle poems,
puzzle poems,
make us stop and think.

An Easy Puzzle

*I'm not on your desk,
but I should be.
You watched TV
instead of doing me.*

Answer: *Homework.*

7

Emergency

I
can't
wait
a
minute
or
two—

I
have
to
go!
I
really
do!

$$12 \times 12 = ?$$

Ms.
Jones
is
busy
over
there.

She
said
to
stay
right
in
my
chair!

I'll
raise
my
hand
so
she
might
see—

Oh,
no!
She's
busy
as
can
be!

I
hope
she
sees
me
*really
fast*—

I
just
don't
think
that
I
can
last!

Why,
oh
why,
do
I
have
to
wait?

SSSSSSSSSSSSSSSSSSSSSS

Oh,
horrors!
Now
it
is
TOO
LATE!

*I should
have yelled
"Emergency!"
then left
the class
immediately!*

The Sink and the Toilet Have a Talk

The sink and the toilet
have a talk one day.
The toilet says,
"I'm glad
when kids come here to play."

The sink says,
"Sometimes
students just appear,
to read all the poems
the teacher hangs here."

The toilet says,
"Remember
when the hamster died?
Children hid in here,
and some of them cried."

The sink says,
"Students
sometimes need to rest,
and the bathroom is the place
they like the best."

A Funeral in the Bathroom

Tears in the bathroom,
time to say good-bye
to a chubby little fish—
we called him Pudgy Pie.

We could almost hear him say,
"This fish food is so good!
It's *my* ice cream and pizza pie!"
Oh, how he loved his food!

But here beside the toilet,
we try to decide.
Did Pudgy eat too much?
Is this why he died?

We place him on the water
amid a gentle hush.
Then we push the handle,
and the toilet starts to flush.

Pudgy's back in water.
Oh, how he loved to swim!
And here in the toilet,
he takes his final spin.

One last exciting whirl,
before he must move on.
And then in one giant gulp,
our little fish is gone.

Looking in the Mirror at an **A**

I've had a life of Bs and Cs
and far too many low-class Ds.

But today,
I can finally say,
the guy in the mirror
is an

Blabbermouth

Blabbed the secret
in the hall,
every word—
told it all.
Announced it
to everyone,
then realized
what I'd done.
Ran to the bathroom,
tears in my eyes,
stood by the sink,
started to cry.
Looked in the mirror,
east to west,
realized I'd
made a mess.
Looked again,
north to south,
saw the face
of a

Blabbermouth.

Trapped!

I'm trapped in the bathroom.
What rotten luck!
Right at recess,
with a door that is stuck.

My teacher and
the custodian too,
are trying to figure out
what to do.

I'd climb out the window,
but it's too high.
If only I were
a bird that could fly.

Or a piece of paper
that's perfectly flat—
I'd slip under the door,
and get out like that.

Or something so small
I could flush me away,
and go whirling around
for a swim today.

Or a magician
with a magical spell,
Abracadabra—
and all is well.

If I could be
SUPERKID
just for a day,
I'd be going outside
with my friends to play.

Instead I'm trapped,
with the door that's stuck,
right at recess,
what awful luck!

Crying in the Bathroom

I'm crying in the bathroom
and need to take a break,
from a heart that is too heavy
and a head that always aches.

I'm crying in the bathroom
for a life that lost its glue—
Mommy's house,
Daddy's place,
pulled apart in two.

I'm crying in the bathroom
where I can be alone,
away from kids and teachers
and the sadness of my home.

The Puzzle Poem on the Bathroom Wall

My head's
in a muddle,
and I can't find
the puzzle
in this puzzle of a poem.

The Perfectionist in Class 4B

I'm
the
perfectionist
in
class
4B.

I
always
cross
my
i's
and
dot
my
t's!

On St. Patrick's Day

Right after
the leprechaun was seen,

the water
turned a sludgy, slimy

G R E E N!

The Note on the Bathroom Wall

Someone wrote a note on the wall.
I wonder who it could be.
Someone wrote a note on the wall,
and they signed it,

Me.

Someone wrote a note on the wall
with my dark blue pen.
Someone wrote a note on the wall—

sigh!

Someone who loves Ben.

Laughing Machines

Jarrod says my nose
is big enough
for two heads,
so I go to the bathroom
to check.

It is big,
but not that big.
Maybe one and
one-half heads
at the most.

Carlos comes into
the bathroom
while I am squishing
my nose down
with my finger.
He looks in the mirror
and sighs.

"I hate Jarrod!
He says I need a lifeguard
to go to the bathroom
because I'm short enough
to drown in the toilet."

We look at each other
and all of a sudden
we start
to laugh
and laugh
and laugh.

When we finally
go back to class,
my nose is still big,
and Carlos is still short,

but somehow,
we feel so much better.

Always Sick

Before I went
to the hospital,
I hid in the bathroom
and cried.

I'm back with
a horrible secret:

*This time
I could have died.*

The Bathroom Dance

We
  do
    the
      wiggle
        jiggle
          do-si-doh,

bounce
  up
    and
      down
        when
       we
      have
    to
    go,

cross our legs,
    hold our pants—

        we all know

    the Bathroom Dance!

The Bully in the Bathroom

We were in the bathroom,
the bully and I.
He punched me,
I punched him back,

and that's when he cried!

Toilet Paper Thoughts

I wish someone
would write on me,

a puzzle,
a story,
or poetry.

once upon a time there was a beautiful princess who lived in a palace far away...

It Happened in Stall Number Three

It happened in
Stall Number Three,
to a girl named
Anna Lee.

A special charm,
a golden key,
a grandma's gift
of jewelry

slipped off her wrist—
she did not see.
It flushed away
in tragedy.

There is a girl
named Anna Lee
who will not use
Stall Number Three.

The Puzzle Poem by the Sink

There's a poem by the sink,
and it made me stop to think,

really,
really,
think!

Just a little short poem
by the sink.

I Cannot Get My Homework Done

Unless I'm alone
or with someone,
I cannot get
my homework done.

Answer: You are always either alone or with someone.

You Forgot to Flush Me!

Flush,
flush,
flush,
I flush all day.
I spend my time
flushing away.

First comes Josh,
then comes Lou,
then comes Chris,
then comes you.

Flush,
flush,
flush,
I flush all day.
I spend my time
flushing away.

Hey!
Get back here!
You forgot to flush!

Surfing in the Bathroom

(inspired by a flood in the boys' bathroom)

I flush the toilet
and hear the crash—

water is flooding,
so I dash

slipping,
sliding,
till I reach the door—

the water
gushes
and rises
some more,

up to my ankles,
then to my knees,

and I am surfing
on bathroom seas.

The water pours
into the hall.

"Emergency!"
the principal calls.

I sail by the kids
in my class

and wave to them
as I go past,

and ride the surf
right out the door

and all the way
to Singapore,

where I write
this very poem

and take a plane
to fly back home.

The Boy in the Girls' Bathroom

I was by the sink,
just trying to think,
when a dog walked in.

I saw the tail,
and started to wail,
"There's a dog in here!"

And then I thought,
"What if it's NOT
the right kind of dog?

"I'll make myself clear
that you can stay here
if you're a girl dog.

"But if you're a boy,
with a name like Roy…
go to the BOYS' bathroom—
NOW!"

There's a Sock in the Toilet

There's a sock in the toilet.
It gave me quite a scare.
There's a sock in the toilet.
How did it get in there?

There's a sock in the toilet.
It should be in a shoe.
There's a sock in the toilet.
I've detective work to do.

There's a sock in the toilet.
I'll check Jim and Rick.
There's a sock in the toilet.
I'll check Tim and Nick.

There's a sock in the toilet.
I'm searching like a hawk.
There's a sock in the toilet—

AHA!

Benjamin,
where's your other sock?

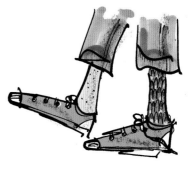

The Puzzle on Stall Number Six

Our teacher is up to
arithmetic tricks.
Just look at this puzzle
on Stall Number Six.

**Add Me Up
and I Am ME**

*Add me up,
and I'm still ME.
You can add me
two times,
or a trillion and three.
Add me up,
and I'm still
ME!*

Answer: *No matter how many times you add up zero, the answer will always be zero.*

Down the Sewer

I'd rather go down the sewer
than hear,
"DETENTION
today."

So I'm heading
to the bathroom
to flush myself away.

Washing My Hair in the Bathroom after Recess

A bird dropped a dropping,
right in midair—
Yuck!
Ooooooooh!
Gross!
Poooooooh!

It landed in my hair!

Bathroom Pass

Grab the pass,
come on, Paul.
Let's take a walk
down the hall.

The water fountain—
watch it drip.
It's your turn,
so take a sip.

Peek in the clinic.
The nurse is there.
She's checking for lice
in Richard's hair.

Kids are running
in the gym.
I'll sneak a look
and wave to Kim.

The principal's office—
don't make a sound.
Take a peek
in the Lost and Found.

34

There's the classroom
with the cockroach pet.
The kids call it
Sweet Juliet.

The teachers' room—
peek if you dare.
They're always eating
treats in there!

Into the bathroom
to play with the soap.
What's on the sink?

An envelope?

It might be important,
you know,
so off to the secretary
we go.

We drop it off,
now back to class.

OH,
how we love

the bathroom pass!

Germs

It was about germs…that TV show.
The bathroom has a zillion, you know.
They jump on your hands—and they grow!

Now I always flush…
with my toe!

Hit-and-Run

There was a
hit-and-run
in my class.
Shelley hit me
with a karate chop,
and I ran
to the one place
she couldn't go—

the BOYS' BATHROOM!

Dancing in the Bathroom

I love the bathroom
where I can set free
the divine ballerina
inside of me.

Oh, I can hear the music
as I dress in dazzling pink!
I'm twirling!
I'm pirouetting!
on the stage beside the sink.

The stalls in the bathroom
begin to disappear
into crowds of people
who stand up and cheer.

I still hear the clapping
as I head back to class,
ready for
some reading,
some writing,
and some math.

Broken Toilet

The custodian put
the sign on the wall:

BROKEN TOILET.
DON'T USE THIS STALL!

Broken Toilet:

*The kids aren't allowed
to come in here.
I need the plumber
and all his gear.*

(Joey walks into the bathroom.)

Joey:

I think the toilet
isn't broken at all.
Watch me go
right into this stall.

Broken Toilet:

*Read the sign.
Can't you see?
YOU NEED TO GET
AWAY FROM ME!*

Joey:

It's flushing,
it's flushing,
it's flushing away.
It's fl—

Joey:

HELP!
Water is flooding
everywhere,
and I'm drenched down
to my underwear.

Broken Toilet:

Why did he do it?
He must be a fool.
Why don't kids listen
when they're in school?

Mirror, Mirror on the Wall

Emily: Mirror, mirror on the wall,
          who's the loveliest of all?

Mirror: The mirror, mirror tells you true,
          that the loveliest part of you
          is always hidden from my view.

And you (Jennifer),

and you (Katie),

and you (Samantha),

and all the others too.
The lovely is inside of you.

A High Five on the Wall

The sink and the toilet
heard me yell, "Yay!
I did it!
I did it!
I did it today!

"I passed the scary spelling test,
went from dumb to smart.
I can spell!
I can spell!
I've finally learned the art!"

I giggled in the mirror,
slapped a high five on the wall,
did a twist,
did a twirl,
then skipped into the hall.

Our Toilet Flushes on Its Own

Our toilet flushes on its own
in the bathroom all alone

at one o'clock every day—
makes us wonder if ghosts play

in the bathroom while we write.
Are they hiding there in white?

Are they giving us a sign
when they flush right on time?

Are they saying loud and clear,

*We may be gone,
but we're still here?*